JAKE'S BIRTHDAY

Rob Lewis

"When is my birthday, Mum?" asked Jake.
"In two weeks," said Mum.

"Too long," groaned Jake.
"Don't worry, the time will soon pass," said Mum.
"Anyway, it's Henry's birthday first, then it's . . ."
But Jake wasn't listening.
"I will have a cake and a party and cards
and friends and presents," he said excitedly.

Every morning, Jake waited for the postman to arrive,
but no birthday cards came.
Then at last the postman brought a lot of letters
in brightly coloured envelopes.

"Those are for me," said Henry, taking them from Jake.
Jake was horrified.
"Hey! Henry's got my cards!" he wailed.
"It's **my** birthday today," said Henry.
"It's not fair!" yelled Jake.
"Henry mustn't have a birthday before me."

Henry opened some of his presents.
There was a new bike from his mum and dad,
a bat from Uncle Stanley
and some roller skates from his grandparents.

"I want presents," said Jake.
"You'll get some, on your birthday," said Mum.
"I want my birthday NOW!" said Jake crossly.

"Come with me," said Mum.
"I've bought a present for you to give to Henry.
You can help me wrap it up."

Jake helped to wrap up the shiny new football.
He would have liked it for himself.
"Now take it downstairs and give it to Henry,
while I tidy up," said Mum.

But Jake didn't give the present to Henry.
He hid it in his wardrobe.

In the afternoon, some of Henry's friends
came to his birthday party.
"Come and say hello," said Mum to Jake.
"I want my friends," said Jake.
"Your friends will come to your birthday party
next week," said Mum.

"I want my birthday NOW," said Jake.
"That's enough. You can still have fun
on Henry's birthday," said Mum.

"There are all your favourite games,
then there's a lovely birthday tea,
and a huge chocolate birthday cake."

Jake liked the sound of the birthday cake.
"I'll try to have fun," he said weakly.

And by teatime he found that he **had** been having fun.

Afterwards they played more games – Follow the Leader,

and Hide and Seek.

Then they paddled in the lake.

After Henry's friends had gone home, Jake rushed upstairs.

"Here's your present," said Jake.

"I wondered where that had gone," said Mum.

"I was saving it," said Jake.

"It's great," beamed Henry.

Jake was pleased that Henry liked his present.

"Will you play football with me?" asked Henry.
"Yes!" said Jake.

"Bedtime!" said Mum.
"Henry's birthday **was** fun," said Jake.
"But now is it my birthday?"

"Nearly," said Mum.

"But first it's Daddy's birthd…"

But Jake wasn't listening.
"I will have cake and a party and cards . . ."